After the Prodigal Returns

A TALE OF THREE PHONE CALLS

JEFF BRETHAUER

Copyright © 2010 Jeff Brethauer
All rights reserved.

ISBN: 1451579837
ISBN-13: 9781451579833

Dedications

To my wife Linda, an incredible life partner and God's greatest gift to me

To Mark, blessed son and living example of a heart that loved deeply, even in times of great pain

To Amy, Dave, Debbie, and Terry who were the first to give of themselves in reviewing this book

To countless family and friends who allowed God to use them to wrap His loving arms around us

Most importantly to our Heavenly Father, whose presence and grace throughout continues to be the true source of our strength, peace and comfort until the day when all will become one in Christ (Deuteronomy 31:8; Matthew 11:28-30)

MR. "M"

Last night I looked back in to see you
after we spoke
And as I gazed upon your sitting form,
As if in a dream having just awoke

I thought of the times we have lost to your
friend Mr. "M"
Sadness crept over my heart,
Along with tears that were hard to stem

I wonder why it is so hard for me to
communicate my love to you?
And I wonder why it is so easy for you
to choose something else to do?

I just know that whatever I say seems
to end up in a problem
And the times we could have had
All seem to go to Mr. "M"

I love you son, Dad
(Written 10/2/05)

* Mr. "M" = marijuana

CONTENTS

Preface ix

The First Call 1

The Second Call 27

The Third Call 57

The Last Call 65

Preface

One night in 2005, God spoke to me in a dream about writing a book reflecting His love and faithfulness in bringing our lost son, Mark, back home to us and the challenges we faced seeking to reconnect as a family. As I started to write the book, I shared portions with my wife Linda and with Mark. The writing of this family history soon became a group effort, but quickly stalled as we reached portions of the narrative that brought many old and buried hurts stingingly to the raw surface of our slowly healing hearts. I felt that God was telling me to put it on the shelf for a season because as a family we were not ready to move forward. At this time Mark was feeling much more like the villain in the story than a means of God reflecting His grace to a family that had suffered much over the past ten-plus years. I now understand the reason that He had me wait. The full story had not yet been written. Mark passed away February 15, 2006. It took another two years before I felt God speaking to me to once again pick up the pen and share of His mighty love and faithfulness to this family._

The beginning of this narrative has its roots in three very different and challenging phone calls. Each of these calls would be the spark God used to take this family through many tough decisions, heartbreaks, and eventually to the healing balm of His grace. This journey would have been impossible without God's presence reflected in countless ways as Linda, Mark, and I traveled the course of separation, tough love, restoration, loss, and eternal promise. Though sad in many parts, this is, above all, a story of one family's victory in the face of the challenges of a hurting world by the great and ever faithful love and grace of God.

the First CALL

The first call came one afternoon in July 1994 when I was at work pouring over the many deliverables soon due. The loud, almost angry ringing of the phone on the crowded corner of my desk startled me out of my worried concentration. The voice on the other end of the receiver was full of fear and panic. It was Linda; she had just concluded an encounter with our son that she never expected to have in a million years. Mark had confronted her in an angry and threatening manner demanding money for his fast-growing habit. This was no longer that little boy that we bounced on our knees and for whose future we had such lofty dreams.

Before I share what occurred, let me explain some events in our family that brought us to this point of a heart-rending decision. We had been going through a very difficult time with Mark ever since I was laid off due to a corporate merger. The merger forced us to take a job in another state as Mark was preparing to enter into his senior year at a private high school, which he had attended since first grade. This was to have been a time of sharing all of the accumulated joys wrapped up into ending one season of life and entering a new phase of budding adulthood, with close friendships developed over the past eleven years. Now the memories of these much-anticipated magic moments of passage were ripped away from him through events far beyond his control. This disappointment turned into a deep-seeded anger; there was no one to blame, except maybe life itself. Mark angrily and eagerly took hold of anyone or anything that would comfort him and support his inner turmoil.

This anger led to poor performance in his senior year at his new high school and a fast-mounting frustration at trying to fill the gaps of lifelong friendships, now seemingly forever left behind. Mark, with much parental and teacher support, barely graduated that final year. During this time he began his journey into the sad and barren world of drugs. Mark still lived at home and worked sporadically at a multitude of jobs while periodically attending classes at a local junior college. He finally reached the point where he refused to attend class at all. Mark had completely lost his desire to continue any pursuit apart from feeding his ever-growing habit.

Often Mark would not come home until the wee hours of the breaking dawn. Linda and I would spend countless hours in prayer, waiting anxiously, staring longingly out of the quarter-paned window in our second-floor spare bedroom. We would listen for the sound of the soft whining engine of his car to pull into the driveway. Once we heard it, somewhat comforted that we had survived another day, Linda and I would quietly slip back into our own bedroom, able to get some measure of sleep to face whatever trials sure to come with the new dawn. We were in a battle for the life of our son and we were floundering, at a loss as to what to do. We had tried reasoning with him, but would quickly resort to cautiously applied forms of discipline, punishments, threats, counseling, and any other possible strategy that would break the momentum of this downward spiral threatening to destroy our family. We were in constant prayer, engaging every friend and prayer warrior we knew to petition our Heavenly Father for the answers we so desperately needed.

Then, one night we heard a hard, heavy knock at the front door. It was one of those knocks that frightfully echoed loudly of something ominous. As we anxiously opened the door, there stood our twenty-one-year old son accompanied by two large men in blue uniforms. Mark was all disheveled and covered with glass embedded in his clothing and hair. He had intentionally driven his car off the exit ramp into a shallow, wooded ravine. Early the following morning, as Linda and I were cleaning out the scattered remains of the crumpled trunk of his tiny red Honda hatchback, we found a spiral notebook containing some very revealing and disturbing notes left to family and friends about his planned "suicide" and desire to join his alternative rock idol, Kurt Cobain (lead singer for Nirvana who had committed suicide a few months previously).

Finding this notebook and its despairing missives broke our hearts. We knew Mark was struggling with a myriad of conflicting emotions, but until this point we had attributed them to the forced relocation and the normal confusion and anger of growing up, finding that real life was far different from childhood dreams. At this point, we began to realize how deeply drugs had gripped his heart and become the healing solace for his hurting soul. Mark's attempt at taking his life was a loud cry for the help he so desperately wanted yet rejected. He had left his seatbelt fastened, a sign that he had not yet truly given up. It seemed he was frantically looking for answers to this hurt deep within himself that would simply not go away. Linda and I had trouble figuring out how to respond to this cry, and it resulted in years of further family pain and separation. Except for the grace of God in the midst of this darkness, Linda and I would never have found strength needed to walk the hard path to restoration. We would have eventually given up in total defeat. But this was not God's plan for us; we were embarking on a journey to battle for a relationship with our son. An as we traveled this path, we would learn the precious truths that God is a healer and a restorer. This battle took over ten years and would end in a way none of us could ever have imagined.

On and on and on we went until that hot, sweaty July afternoon when I received that fateful call from Linda that would set in motion events changing each of us forever. Linda called me in a fearful panic because she had just finished a terrifying confrontation with Mark, who was desperate for money to feed his ever growing need. For the first time, she was deeply disturbed for her safety (in later years Mark would cry when we shared this encounter with him). This was the last straw for me. I could no longer stand by seeing Linda threatened and hoping that Mark would come to his senses without some form of "tough love" response. I rushed out of the office and drove home in a hazy mental fog of anger and frustration. At the time I had no idea of what I was going to find, let alone what I was going to say or do.

Crowding my mind were thoughts of that little blond haired, mischievous, blue-eyed munchkin that would ride my shoulders saying, "Dad, I love you." I asked myself, *Where have you gone?* Mixed with these thoughts was anger about the night before, when Mark ignored my request to have a serious conversation about being more responsible for his life's decisions. He did not come home until late that night, resulting in a very unpleasant confrontation. I had written in my journal that night, *Father, I am so frustrated with Mark, particularly with his rapidly deteriorating attitude.* In ever-increasing frequency, the sad thought crossed my mind that the time was fast approaching to firmly demand that he move out. This slowly made its way from my head to my heart, where I ached so desperately to see that little boy again. Unfortunately, for that to happen we had to turn loose of Mark and totally entrust him into the hands of God. Mark had to be allowed to "come to the end of himself" (just as with the prodigal son whose story Jesus shared with parents so many years ago) and rediscover God's love in that process. Tough love is just that, "tough." You can read all kinds of books and speak to others who have experienced it, but there is no handbook for taking that first step. It's scary and it hurts to the very core of your being. These thoughts were churning in my heart as I pulled into the driveway determined to do what needed to be done for all of our sakes.

I barely remember rushing into the house and climbing the stairs to Mark's bedroom where we faced each other with the bleak understanding that we had run out of time. Mark actually took the ultimatum with a measure of emotional relief. We had finally brought all of the lies, deception, and frustration to a conclusion. He agreed that it was critical for him to move out by the end of the week before the tensions that were rupturing this family took some more serious form. Saturday morning came quickly; without much fanfare, Linda and I let go of our son, entrusting him more fully than ever into The Father's hands. It was July 16, 1994, with arms around each other and in silent tears that we turned loose of our precious son for what would be eight years and twenty-nine days of separation, sporadic contact, and desperate prayers. Truly as with the prodigal child of old, the young son had claimed his inheritance and entered a world that wanted nothing less than to destroy him. And like the father of so long ago, we had to let him go, placing him into the loving hands of our Heavenly Father.

Mark left home and moved into an aging, paint-peeling rental house near the local campus area with several members of his new circle of friends. The first test came in less than two weeks. I was speaking with Mark about returning to work and found out that he had made no effort to secure a means of getting to and from his job. He had no idea of what he was going to do, and was playing that tried and true game that he had used so often over the years: waiting for Mom and Dad to rush to the rescue. We wanted so much to do just that, but knew in our hearts that Mark had to start working out these problems himself or he would never learn to take responsibility for his choices. Even if he lost his job, which I had helped him to secure with my own employer, we had to let him go. It is so hard to be a parent and watch your child suffer because of his foolishness and rebellion. Daily we had to place Mark into the loving hands of our Heavenly Father. It hurt so much!

True to form, Mark did lose his job as he continued his downward spiral. A few weeks later he called Linda, not to see how we are doing or to wish me a happy birthday (two days past), but to secure a ride to the unemployment office. He didn't care that Linda had been hurt at work. Mark's overriding interest was finding ways to support his growing addiction. This destructive desire was fast wrapping itself around his heart and squeezing out everything that threatened to get in its way. Linda and I felt so much like utter failures as parents as we prayed for the strength to leave him in God's hands and for his heart to be softened. We wanted our son back. Now!!

In less than two weeks we received another call from Mark. His troubles had quickly moved from bad to worse. He and his buddies had gotten into a situation where they each owed some local bad guy $500; if he was not paid immediately there would be bodily harm inflicted. I had been praying to meet with Mark for coffee, just to talk with him (no agenda), but I had not expected God to act so quickly or under such dire circumstances. As I met with Mark and his friends I could see fear written plainly on each of their young faces. No sign of party here. Again the urge to dash right in and rescue Mark was at the forefront of my heart, but I felt a check in my spirit to go home and pray first. Linda and I prayed and wrestled with the situation through the night and felt God directing us to call the parents of the other boys. I contacted one parent who gave me some additional background and found out that he had sent this man to confront the young partiers to scare reality into them about their dangerous and foolish path. Once again, God had guided our unsteady steps to entrust our son into His protective arms.

Mark then spent the next night at home because he and his friends were forced to move out of their campus area crash pad. The following day, it quickly became evident that we were still frustrating each other with almost every other sentence and that the original idea to allow him a week at home to get his plans in order would not work at all. Given a foot in the door, Mark would quickly manipulate us to make it a long country mile. We were so disheartened, particularly at seeing Mark show no sense of personal responsibility, thought of God, or concern for the impact that this was having on Linda and me. God kept us on our knees and somehow gave us peace in the midst of the brewing storm.

As summer drifted into fall and fall faded into winter, sliding slowly into the new year, we became somewhat accustomed to the constant ups and downs of caring for Mark. We helped him replace his wrecked car, though he only repaid us half of what he had promised. We would go from rare times of closeness and communication to prolonged periods of deafening silence and concern. This continual seesaw of emotions was quickly wearing on Linda and me. Out of our love and fear for Mark, we found ourselves taking it out on each other in numerous ways.

Mark, too, was suffering as the words of this song he had written evidence:

"BLEND"

Sitting here, drifting away
Thinking silently, about yesterday
And the day before, and the day before
Oh the days, how they seem to repeat themselves.
Over and over again,
A pattern of the same,
Like the repeating rain,
Existing in "Neverland"
Seeking the "Promised Land"
I've about given up hope.

(Mark Brethauer)

I had a deeply disturbing dream concerning Mark's and my relationship, focusing on the root causes of the hardness of his heart that had seemed to have overtaken him in these last few challenging years. My dream carried me back to a very difficult time in our marriage where my selfishness and spiritual pride did much damage to Linda and our relationship, deeply hurting Mark in the midst. It is so easy to forget certain times in your life when you have moved past them without realizing that others wounded during that period may still have some unresolved hurts. God was moving me to have a heart-to-heart conversation with Mark to ask his forgiveness of my foolish actions of years ago.

Mark's spirit needed healing and often letting go of the past (forgiving) is the first step. I discussed the dream and proposed conversation with Linda and she agreed. A week and a half later, we were all sitting together having another trying conversation in which Mark blamed everyone and everything else for his problems, including another job he had recently lost. He did not like hearing how his actions were affecting others and became quite defensive. At that point, God gave me the opportunity to confess to Mark how my thoughtless and selfish actions had severely hurt our family several years before. I then asked his forgiveness. This opened the door for some honest dialogue as we discussed his growing up and life's disappointment. Mark claimed he had forgiven me, but it was evident to see that there was much more work for God to do in healing his heart. "Oh Heavenly Father, my heart cries out for my son; please minister your unconditional love to his precious soul!"

As the weeks passed by, we entered into a period of uneasy truce with Mark where we all tried to get along by communicating with mutual respect and spending time together with no preplanned agenda. Mark and I would meet to play chess, which opened doors for Mark to openly express himself. God helped me to quietly listen and not respond with my well-meaning but ineffective comments. This was very hard for me. Mark shared his frustrations while living at home: the need to find a church that he felt comfortable in; how we (Linda and I) don't listen and needed to better value his friends and passion for music. Though Mark was trying hard to be more open about his beliefs and plans, he was totally silent about the deeper bondage that drugs were steadily claiming without pity, silently robbing him of life's joy. His struggles with self value were keeping him from being honest with himself and others as he struggled to find peace within. He was following, without heed, that dangerous downward road of destruction, guided by that beguiling pied piper, "Mr. M."

"UNTITLED"
Looking in the mirror
I stare into my eyes
Quickly turning away
From my outer disguise
Hatred toward myself
And a feeling of regret
For the lack of loyalty
And goals never kept.

(Mark Brethauer)

Mark, once again, moved back in with us for who knew how long. As before things did not work as he envisioned. With jobs coming and going, friends falling in and out of his life, and still no sense of taking up life's responsibilities, he focused all efforts on achieving the next high with his only true buddy "Mr. M." In spite of this, we could not refuse allowing him to stay with us until he was situated enough to move back out. Truly, love is blind! It was not long before all the old tensions were ripping away at each of us. Linda and I felt a growing bitterness with Mark; in trying to fight this anger we followed the old pattern of taking out our frustrations on each other. In one instance, I found myself extremely angry with both Linda and Mark for spending $1,500 in car repairs that we had not agreed upon providing. This was additionally challenging because times were financially tight for us. How was Mark ever going to learn to take responsibility for his own life if we kept rushing in like the Red Cross to rescue him? Satan was truly using the love we felt for our son to tear deeply at our marriage and family. To help fight this battle, Linda and I began to spend more time in joint prayer and seeking comfort and direction from God's word together.

Once again we told him that he would have to leave and once again he agreed that it was necessary for the benefit of us all. Mark decided to move in with a friend of his who was experiencing very similar issues with his parents. In talking with this boy's parents, we agreed that this might be the best thing for the both of them. It could help jumpstart the maturing process and provide a fresh start. Linda and I again agreed to take the risk of cosigning for Mark and his friend with the agreement of the collaborating parents guaranteeing their son's portion of the lease.

A month and a half later, I found myself confronting Mark again over his total disregard of both financial and relational responsibilities. Mother's Day had come and gone without a card or a call or any type of recognition from the boy for whom Linda had sacrificed so much over the years. This, more than anything else, sent me past the boiling point. He found it easy to show up at our house whenever he felt like it and expect Linda to still do his laundry. Also, he would scrounge the cupboards for food items that he refused to buy, so that he had money for his

THE FIRST CALL

own pleasures. On top of these issues, he was letting his car payments slip past due and we, as cosigners, would have to take care of the delinquent bills. He seemed like a stranger to us. We loved him so much and knew we had to let him be completely responsible for his actions, yet found ourselves time and again reaching back in to rescue him. *Would this crazy emotional seesaw ever end? Oh God, we need you so desperately!*

It took only a couple of weeks to make clear to us that we were far from the lowest point that Mark's selfish choices would take this family. We found out that he had begun to take his addiction to a new level. He had now gone into "farming": growing his own marijuana plants in the basement of his apartment, for which we had cosigned. We found out about this through my nephew who had come to stay with us for a week. Mark, thinking it was cool, not only bragged to him about what he was doing, but took him on a private guided tour of his "farm." Needless to say, this not only embarrassed Linda and me before our family, but we were painfully realizing how his love for drugs was consuming his every conscious thought with no regard for the impact on himself, let alone others. As we sought to talk with him about how his actions were truly getting out of control, he could only make empty promises. He continued to play games with us, God, and, most critically, himself.

The very next week, Mark called us to ask for rent money; for once, we totally refused to come running to his rescue. He was shocked that we were not madly rushing in to meet this "Mark made" emergency. He was so used to manipulating our emotions into getting him out of self-created jams that he did not know what to do when we refused to be drawn in once again. Only by prayer and God's strength were Linda and I able to stay united and cling to our shaky resolve. *Why does it seem to bother us so much more than it does Mark? Father, without your strength we can't do this!*

The hidden truth was that all of this did bother Mark, but he found it hard to share what was really going on inside because of the wicked combination of drugs and pride. He was lost. True to form, my birthday came and went without any word from Mark. I just buried the hurt in my heart and explained it away as the thoughtless actions of a selfish son who was squandering his life and his future, praying that someday my prodigal would return. This was far from what was actually churning inside Mark's soul. He did care, as these poetic words found in his notebook so painfully reflect:

> It's my daddy's birthday
> And I see what I have done
> How can my daddy love me
> Because he knows what I've become
> I'm watching him grow old
> Aged with years of pain
> Years passed so quickly
> And only memories remain
> Is he proud of me
> After I shamed his name

THE FIRST CALL

> How could he let me
> Come home again
> Love beyond me, seemed to come so easily
> Love beyond me, takes the weight from the guilty
> Undeserving son; takes his fortune to town
> Fortunate son; spreads his worth around
> No money, no friends
> Unconditional love, depends on no one
> Won't you let me come home again?
> I promise, I promise
> (Mark Brethauer - 8/16/1996)

It would take another six years for Mark to act on these words and, like the father of the prodigal son in the Bible, we, in painful hope, waited on the porch to catch that first glimpse of him coming over the horizon.

A month and a half later, I was at work when I received an angry phone call from the management office of Mark's apartment complex. They demanded that I bring them two month's rent plus late charges and NSF check fees within the next two hours. Mark had wasted no time in squandering this latest opportunity to take ownership for his life. He and his buddy had a falling out causing everything to fall behind as both pursued their destructive habit for only one love (Mr. M). Linda and I decided that the best course of action was to exercise the buyout clause on the lease and put the problem back into Mark's irresponsible lap.

Mark was evicted, forced to give up "farming" and destroy his precious crop. Truly God was trying to get his attention while protecting him from the hard consequences of the deceptive world of which he had become such a captive. He asked to move back in with us to get himself resituated. Linda and I realized that this had to be for a very short period otherwise we would be back to square one in supporting his destructive lifestyle. We agreed to allow him no more than thirty days to stay with us and regroup. God, in His faithfulness, provided the perfect place that very week, "right on time." We located an inexpensive house with shared living quarters that would require Mark to work in unity and cohabitation with strangers. When we met with the landlady and the house members for an interview; she offered Mark the room on the spot. We accepted and wrote a check just as quickly, committing that he would move in the very next morning. The thirty-day window had quickly shrunk down to three days. As I looked over to Mark, I saw the shock written all over his face as he realized that there would be no cushy stay back with Mom and Dad. Once again our hearts went out to him and the pain that we knew was buried deep within. Once again we knew the piercing hurt of that often quoted phrase, "tough love."

It did not take long before Mark moved out of this forced living arrangement. Thus began several years of a twisted journey of living in a multitude of drug houses surrounding the local college campus. Mark, in his anger, began to withdraw deeper into his shadowy world of drugs and disillusionment. During this same period, Linda and I entered a season where we would be severely challenged in every area of life. Linda's parents became so ill that we had to sell all they owned and move them into assisted living quarters located a few miles from where we were currently living. At the same time Linda was injured twice at work requiring reconstructive neck and foot surgery combined with the real possibility of losing her job. My position was also being threatened through a corporate merger which raised the risk of being forced to move out of state if I wanted to stay employed within my profession. On top of this, my beloved grandmother passed away. Through all of these refining and trying life events, Mark was nowhere to be found. We later realized that God was using these life-altering events to enable us to let go of Mark and truly trust him to the care of our Heavenly Father.

One night, a few months later, I had another vivid dream about Mark. I saw a picture of his exposed heart that brought a cold fear to my soul. It was bound very tightly, almost completely surrounded by some very hard rubber substance, which was gradually turning to stone or metal. Mark had built this growing hardness from the inside out as he created a protection for himself from the hurts of life's relationships (both real and imagined). He was allowing the destructive lies of Satan and the world to cut himself off from all who truly cared; everyone, that is, except his habit, which had become his closest friend. In the midst of this terrible dream, God's soft whisper spoke words of hope into my heart, a gentle voice saying over and over again, "Only love can melt the walls of a hardened and hurting heart." I immediately cried out to God in prayer to give Linda and me such love for our son, a love without condition. We pleaded for the wisdom and courage of heart to live and trust God to bring our lost prodigal home. Though it sure didn't feel like it at the moment, God was working in all of us to do just that!

The months continued to pass and we would see Mark once in a while for coffee or a quick meal. We would listen anxiously for any words of change in our son's heart. Most times, there was only that very frustrating self focus, but once in a while he would tell us that someone had challenged him about his lifestyle and returning to the values he once embraced. We continued to wait, watch, pray, and love. As this period in our lives weaved it's slowly evolving path, Linda and I found ourselves facing two huge life events that would further rock our world and refine our faith. Linda's dad, who had been battling cancer for the last few years, passed away suddenly on the morning of our twenty-eighth wedding anniversary. We were so glad that we had moved her parents to be near us and were blessed to be able to spend so much time with them during this tragic season. Along with this heartache came the news that I would be expected to move several hundred miles away if I wanted to maintain my current employment. Mark did attend his grandfather's funeral but was oblivious to the struggles we had been going through on so many fronts.

A couple of months later, I resigned from my current employer and took another job with a company in a nearby city about a hundred miles away. This was the first time

THE FIRST CALL

since Mark began his torturous journey that Linda and I were not able to be in immediate reach in his times of need. Again, God was moving in our lives to entrust Mark more fully to Him. Mark now had to face his life choices with a much more distant lifeline.

Mark had become firmly entrenched in the drug scene that flourished all over the greater campus area. Mark moved from house to house and friend to friend as he and his ever-changing circle of companions encouraged each another down their mutual road of destruction. Mark had become not only a user but also a dealer; this habit fully consumed his life. He also became involved in an emotionally volatile relationship with a female that lasted for several years. Linda and I always tried to stay connected with our son and let him know how much we loved him. We never wanted to close permanently the path that would lead back home. He continued to take us for granted as he ever-so-gradually grew into a man, lost in a culture that had but one agenda: to totally destroy him. When we would meet with Mark and his friends, it was so disheartening to see how they encouraged one another in this fantasy world of self-destruction and delusion.

I was able to spend one cold October evening with Mark and he was visibly disturbed at the direction that his life had taken. For once, I just sat still and listened. I did not quickly jump in with that "if you would just listen to me," full of implied judgment, fatherly advice. He was shaken because he was about to lose his apartment and had no idea of what to do next. Mom and Dad were not a mere trip across town any longer and he was feeling very much alone. As we shared precious moments that night, I saw creeping into view, in ever so fleeting glimpses, that young man who the drugs had masked for so long. We actually ended the evening praying together and I left his presence with the first sense of hope in a very long time.

Within a few weeks, Mark did find a new place (just as we had prayed). With emergency of the moment gone, so was his desperation and openness. As Mark quickly slipped back into his old patterns, my new job began to develop some challenges as the business unit was put up for sale. Linda's job also was in jeopardy through a corporate restructure. We spent most of the year in a state of nervous flux as God worked in our lives to provide new positions within our current employments. The biggest result was another major move. This time it was almost six hundred miles farther away from Mark. Truly God was working in all of us to create the necessary separation that would finally bring Mark to the end of himself!

As we began our transition out of state, God moved to once again shake Mark's world in an attempt to awaken him from this horrendous nightmare of which he had become such a lost, wandering participant. Mark and his girlfriend were forcibly evicted from their apartment with all of their meager belongings strewn carelessly all over the front lawn and curb. Mark called us in a panic. It was becoming painfully clear to him that it was up to him to face the problems that he had created for himself.

THE FIRST CALL

The eviction stirred Mark to take steps to honestly address going forward in life. He began calling us much more often for advice or just to talk. We worked with him to secure admittance and grant monies for attending a local trade school. We agreed to partner with him as he began taking these giant steps on the road back home. We secured funding and Mark passed admittance testing down to the last math exam. Just when all appeared to be coming together in that long-awaited return to the son we knew and longed for, the bottom once again dropped out. It was beyond Mark's power to stay committed to this new course in the long run. With the situations in his life gradually taking on a form of normality and hope, he opened the door once again for his "ever at the doorstep" friend "Mr. M." He completely ceased all efforts in attending school and dived head-long, body and soul, into that drug life that was sucking out all hope of a positive future like a plunger to a toilet bowl.

It was just before Thanksgiving when we received another distress call for help from Mark. He needed money for new eyeglasses and car repairs. Linda and I drew the line and informed him that we would cover his glasses only and that would be this year's Christmas present. He seemed to accept this. We went forward with setting up the eye exam and obtaining the new glasses. Two hours later, I received another call from Mark informing that his car was already perched atop a hoist and that he had secured a great price to complete the repairs needed. Anger pierced my heart at this blatant attempt at emotional manipulation. I bit my tongue as I, in a measured but firm response, told him that he would just have tell them to take the car down off the hoist as we would not be paying this time. The quiet on the phone line got very loud; in solemn silence we ended the conversation. With the click of the receiver, a sharp pain shot through my heart. We felt that now we had totally abandoned our beloved son. Would we ever hear from him again? Love hurts!

For the next twenty months, God continued to use challenges and tragedies to refine our faith and strengthen us for what was yet looming over the dark horizon. Looking for some much-needed personal time, Linda and I took a little getaway to focus our attention on us. Two days into this precious time we picked up a very impersonal voice message from a nurse on duty at the home where Linda's mom was living, stating that she had passed away during the night. Once again, we were back in the thick of life's many heartaches. When would this end? Though Linda's mom had been sick on and off for several years, the reality of her death hit all of us extremely hard. It impacted Mark greatly because he had spent many a summer with her and they were very close when he was young. One more time, he strived to put his self-destructive life in order and once again the progress was short-lived, as the seemingly never-ending downward cycle claimed its chokehold on his life.

During this solemn period, I asked a couple of my friends, in a hopeful effort, to make direct contact with Mark to see if he would respond to someone else's voice of life experience. Possibly, he would realize that others had overcome many of the same obstacles that he was facing? They faithfully set up meetings with him over coffee and shared candidly with him the struggles that they had faced in life. With words of stark honesty, they reminded him that there was a way out and he did not have to face the battle alone. Mark was very open and honest in return as he discussed what was going on in his life. The bottom line was that he liked "Mr. M" and was not about to give him up.

Mark and his longtime girlfriend separated. He totally wrecked his car and lost his apartment. We agreed to fly Mark down to see us for some much-needed family reconnect time. During this visit we had great one-on-one conversations and spent many hours over coffee engaged in long and challenging discussions. We could see that Mark truly missed not having us close by, even if for nothing more comforting than being his safety net. We tried to encourage him to completely remove himself from his present environment, which served only to support his destructive lifestyle and move closer to us. Though at times Marks resolve would waver, he still was not able in his heart to let "Mr. M" go. He feared the purposeless path on which he was blindly traveling, but he feared even more a future that would force him to leave his habit behind.

The three of us stayed on this bumpy path of trying to put our family back together though Christmas and into the next year. For the first time in many years, Mark actually sent Linda and me Christmas gifts and cards with wonderful words of love and appreciation. Then the world went silent! The ever-familiar pattern was rearing its ugly, foul face once more. As Linda and I waited and prayed our way through this latest cycle, one more crushing blow came crashing down upon us. My mom, who had gone in for some seemingly routine surgery, found herself on life support with a critical infection. A few days later, with her sons gathered around her in prayer, my mom peacefully left this world for the next. Mark was devastated at the news that his last living grandparent was now gone. He was both broken-hearted and deeply immersed in his habit as he tried to deal with these tragic events. My brothers confronted him and told him point blank that he was killing himself and needed to take steps to deal with his addiction. Mark responded in his typical "I can handle it" attitude and disappeared down the road in determined silence and pride.

We continued on in this strained silence until one hot, humid day in July when in lightening-like suddenness, breaking the early evening stillness, came the "second call." Mark was scared of the death grip that drugs now had on his life and was ready to honestly deal with it. He wanted to come home!

the Second
C A L L

THE SECOND CALL

> Sitting on an unmade bed
> The pictures flowing through his head
> The cigarettes are tasting worse today
> Peace of mind seems so far away
> Reaching for the hopeless land
> Brings a mind set to the end
> Recalling a happier man
> Trying to bring back the past
> Changes come so quickly
> When you're looking the other way
> Mistakes are made.
>
> (Mark Brethauer)

It was mid-July 2002, a little over eight years since we entered that painful and seemingly never-ending path of tough love initiated when our drug-influenced son had threatened Linda in our home. As excited as we were at this much-longed-for cry for help from our precious son, our hearts were also filled with an intense fear of repeating a past that had cut deep wounds into all of our hearts. *Oh God, we so desperately want this to be the hour of our lost sons return. Grant us wisdom as we go forward.* This was our prayer as we sought to join with God in understanding next steps all of us needed to take. We called several drug treatment centers both locally and nationally. Every one of them told us that at the very least, Mark must complete drug detox before we could allow him to move back into our home.

We entered a three-week period of daily calls of desperation from Mark, in-depth conversations with drug treatment counselors, and intense prayer. It was so hard to talk with Mark; with each call, he pleaded for us to drop everything and come take him home. We had to fight fiercely within ourselves to hold on to the tough wisdom of the counselors, who were adamant that he must check himself into a rehab center first. Mark finally understood that nothing was going to happen until he took the first step. He continued in his attempt to manipulate our emotions by promising to check himself into the rehab center, but he always found a reason why he couldn't do it that day. At last in early August Mark took the huge step. The scary thing about being able to check yourself into a clinic is that you can also check yourself out. After a few days, Mark called us from his apartment crying and apologizing at the same time that he just couldn't stay in a place with so many tight restrictions. Mark was addicted to nicotine as well as drugs, and it was beyond him to deal with breaking both dependencies at the same time. If you missed the assigned smoking breaks, you had to wait for the next one. Finally, Mark simply checked himself out and immediately phoned us.

Mark's voice was full of fear when he called because he knew that detox was nonnegotiable. He swore adamantly that he had done no drugs and was completely clean. He begged us to rescue him before he slipped back into the addiction that he was sure would totally destroy him in a matter of days this time. He desperately needed something, someone to have hope in or he would completely give up the fight. Linda and I prayed feverishly for God's immediate guidance. Our son's life was at stake! God, in His infinite faithfulness, quickly gave both of us inner peace that "now" was the time to go retrieve our long-lost son! Again, like the father of the prodigal son, who upon seeing his son appear on the horizon, we ran to meet him. Once Linda and I saw Mark finally truly ready to honestly face his addiction, we immediately raced to embrace our dear son.

On August 12, 2002, Linda and I sped hurriedly and nervously six hundred miles north in the desperate hope that we were doing the right thing? When we arrived at Mark's apartment we found an emaciated shadow of the young man we had seen only a few weeks before. He was so weak that he was barely able to help us with the move. In four hours time, we secured a rental truck with a car tow, sold Mark's second car for cash on the spot, collected all monies owed him by friends, packed all of his meager belongings in the truck, and left town. Truly God was confirming His voice to us two days before that "now" indeed was the time. It was a miracle that the three of us left the old battleground behind with no loose ends. As we headed home in anxious silence and reflection, we wondered: *What would this new future bring? Where was God taking us?* There was also a song of joy and thanksgiving in our hearts! Our son who was lost had now been found! He who was dead is now alive!

The next day, after we arrived home, we saw firsthand the terrible grip that drugs still held on both Mark's body and mind. He began to suffer convulsions from drug withdrawal and had to be taken to the emergency room the next morning. The doctors immediately enrolled him in the state-regulated methadone treatment program. Those first two weeks were filled with much concern and fear, wondering if Mark would stay faithful to the commitment he had made to complete rehab or repeat the old formula that we had become so accustomed to living with? During that time we had many long talks with him over steamy cups of coffee and began the process of reconnecting as a family. We were thrilled to see Mark's total determination to put his broken past behind him and build a new future. These were major steps on his part to put the fears of the unknown aside and step-by-step move forward in life.

For the next few weeks, we continued on, watching Mark gradually regain physical and emotional strength, becoming increasingly more stable with each passing day. He never missed a morning of driving five miles to the local clinic for his daily methadone treatment. He would then come right back home, where we engaged in long, painfully honest conversations about the past along with his plans for going forward in life. Mark would break down in tears when we shared the impact that some of his actions had on us, particularly the sad time when he had threatened Linda and stole some precious coins left to her by her father. He was also greatly bothered at missing out on special moments with grandparents, now gone, and many family holidays, now long past. We spent much time encouraging him to learn from the past, not become lost in it. A new future was now before all of us and we were there to partner with him in taking firm a hold of it. It was not our desire to judge or condemn him; he was doing enough of that himself. What he needed was unconditional love and acceptance (not necessarily agreement).

The fact that Mark was back home with us did not mean that we were free from areas of conflict and challenge. Mark was returning with over eight years of baggage, destructive habits, and life experiences that meshed together to make his sense of right and wrong vastly different from what he had been taught growing up. One area that immediately brought us into conflict was showing respect to Linda and me. He was so conditioned to think of self first that he gave little regard to how careless words and thoughtless actions hurt others. I would often say a quick prayer before addressing Mark, and to his credit he listened and made visible effort to modify his responses. There is no substitute for time, and this family had just entered the early stages of the restoration process.

We found that our most precious family times were going out for a Friday afternoon coffee, Saturday morning breakfast, or brunch after church. We made the main focus of the weekend "family time" and seldom did we allow any other activities to take precedent. Ours was a family that had been given a second chance and did not want to waste a single moment of it. We would anxiously begin the weekend as quickly as I was able to madly race home from work, always seeking excitedly to exit the daily rat race as early as possible on a Friday afternoon. Linda and Mark would already be deeply engaged in some heavy life discussion at the local coffee shop as they constantly glanced all around for my arrival. The three of us would review the triumphs and trials of the week for an hour or so before hastily dispersing for the grocery store, picking up dinner, and rushing home to watch a movie, usually one Mark personally selected.

Mark had only been home a couple of months when the next major test came swooping down upon us. He wanted to take a brief trip back to see his old friends and show them how well he was doing. Waves of panic besieged Linda and I: would this reunion with his party buddies only serve as a speedy conduit to bring all of Mark's hard-won improvements to a crashing halt? We had seen this pattern repeated so many times before. At the end of the day, there was nothing we could really say or do, other than entrust him into our Heavenly Father's loving protection. Mark stayed true to his word; he kept in touch with us continually and came back home having stayed clean the entire time. Truly he was committed to making the life changes that were critical and God was continuing to cover us with His powerful love and faithfulness as we determinedly trekked this winding journey of restoration.

Now that Mark had established some emotional stability in addressing the basic issues of staying clean, facing the fears of change and having a place of refuge from the past, it was time for him to take the next steps of reconnecting with the community that he had left so far behind. Mark's lack of self-esteem and confidence greatly inhibited his taking relational risks of any great degree. He had begun to attend church with us and was introduced to some of our closest friends who were very instrumental in opening the emotional doors to his long locked up heart. We also began the cautious process of integrating Mark back into the greater family without feeling like the proverbial "black sheep." Everyone worked very hard to let him know he was loved and that they were overjoyed to have him back. We took the first true family vacation in almost ten years, during which we balanced time with relatives and much needed "fun time" with just the three of us. It was so great to see Mark renew relationships with aunts, uncles, and cousins. It was so good just to see him laugh again! It was so good to laugh together!

The next major step we took was to work with Mark to find a job. This resolve required Mark to take the personal risk of exposing himself to the sense of rejection that comes with the possibility of being turned down when applying for work. With his still-fragile self-esteem, we had to proceed slowly, but with focused determination. This was a key ingredient in rebuilding his sense of self-worth. As we reached the concluding days at the end of the year following Mark's return, he continued to open up more, involve himself in the lives of others, faithfully keep up his daily treatments, and make one more drug-free trip back to see his friends. Mark had secured a part-time job helping a friend of ours in his painting business. God continued to shower His boundless grace upon this family as each one of us with thankful hearts sought to be one again. The battle was not over, but we had taken major steps. We celebrated our first true family Christmas in years. As the Savior of man was born in that manger so many years ago, giving hope to a lost mankind, so too in that hope, we had the rebirth of our son and our family. Things weren't perfect, but they were great. *Thanks, Father!*

As we entered another year, each of us settled into the long process of going forward in life. We had tough conversations about obtaining a job that would provide a future beyond the sporadic work opportunities that Mark was currently chasing. Tensions would quickly surface if we pushed too aggressively. Linda and I could not forget, for a single moment, how far Mark had come in these last six months. We could not let our own anxious feelings for him cause us to rush Mark through God's healing process. One of Mark's reactions to perceived pressure or judgment was to withdraw deep within and refuse to communicate. As necessary as it was for him to take firm hold of his own life's responsibilities, Linda and I had to constantly reinforce with Mark that home was a refuge, a safe environment where we could be totally transparent with one another without consequence. *Letting go and letting God* became the family prayer as God would peel back the layers of the long-developed protective hardness around Mark's heart.

Gradually, his heart began to thaw as he felt safe in his new home. He began to help around the house, attend church with us, talk more openly of past failures, and express words of love to Linda and me. Frequently, we would conclude deep discussions and raw moments with prayer, knowing we not only had God to thank for bringing us back together, but needed His grace for each critical step going forward in reconciling this family. Mark began to explore going back to school, possibly attending some type of trade school until he could pursue his true love, which was music production. He began to address life in a much more positive light. He continued to work his part-time job, putting in more hours, while aggressively looking for a permanent job with benefits. While he was making these efforts, he faithfully made payments from his meager income for the car that we had just purchased. The car he had brought with him finally "gave up the ghost and passed on to car heaven." Mark was demonstrating a growing sense of personal responsibility through very meaningful ways in all areas of his life.

Another positive sign of Mark's reentrance into the family was his cousin's request that he be an usher in his upcoming wedding. This may seem like a very small thing to get excited about, but to Mark it was huge. This was a sign to him that he was accepted and gave him a chance to show in a "hands on" way that he cared deeply for them as well. Mark took his cousin's trust seriously and helped in every way possible to make this simple beach wedding a special day for the newlyweds. As he involved himself in helping others, Mark experienced an additional hard-won success in overcoming his long-time drug addiction. He was steadily reducing the daily doses of his methadone treatments in the hopes of putting those trips across town every morning far behind him. During this exciting time, another huge victory came for his self-esteem: he was hired for a permanent job, including benefits, with a major international employer. Though only part-time in hours, it required daily attendance and opened the door for future advancement. Truly Mark was beginning to realize that God did indeed have a plan for his life and that plan was to see him have a hope and a purpose. God was showing His faithfulness in so many ways! *Father, we thank you!*

Life was beginning to settle into the calmest routine that we had known in years. Mark was pulling double shifts at every opportunity, continuing the steady reductions in his methadone dosage, and managing his financial obligations responsibly. As we cruised along in this apparent season of peace, we were struck soundly with a vivid reminder that the battle for our son was far from over. Linda was sweeping around our back porch when she spotted some strange plants growing in the midst of the plant beds. There, in inconspicuous innocence, were several little, budding marijuana plants. We confronted Mark. What was he thinking? He was risking his future with his new employer (who conducted random drug tests) as well as putting Linda and me in legal danger. We immediately destroyed the mini crop amid Mark's strong objections. He maintained the popular belief that marijuana was harmless and it helped to calm his troubled spirit. We tried desperately to reason with him that in keeping "Mr. M" around he was leaving the door cracked, dangerously open for the potential of sliding down that slippery slope once more. Indeed, we could never let down our guard, lest complacency lull us to sleep and quickly usher in the terrible repeat of a painful past.

Despite this, Mark was continuing to grow in his job, never missing a shift, and worked hard to pay Linda and I back for the money given him to purchase his car. We continued through the year without much drama and were thankful for the season of calm that God had graciously granted us. During this period, we bought a ping-pong table upon which Mark and I relived the passionate competition we had shared in the long past days of Mark's teen years. As we played these matches, Mark and I had great times of mutual sharing. These were special times of just plain, simple enjoyment of each other's presence. Mark was also beginning to grow stronger in his confidence in relationship-building as he spent precious time with family and friends. We shared Thanksgiving this year with a young man from India who was to become a very close friend of Mark's, as they shared a great passion for music. Christmas marked the completion of over sixteen months of reconnecting as a family since that hot summer day when we had brought Mark, in fearful hope, back home with us. The precious time, gift sharing, and Christmas dinner with friends made a wonderful exclamation point of God's grace to this family. With hearts full of joy, Linda and I thanked God not only for the awesome gift of His son, but for the special gift of our dear son as well. *Thank you, Father!*

We began 2004 with thankful hearts wondering what surprises were coming our way. True to form, there were many changes in store for us as we sought to join with God in doing life as a restored family. Through a series of miracles, God made it possible to sell our home and purchase another that more adequately met our current needs. The new place had complete living quarters with a finished kitchen in the basement. This meant that Mark would have some space to call his own for the first time since he returned home. There was even plenty of room for his beloved Meg (a precious border collie/shepherd mix he had raised since birth, the runt of the litter, who was disowned by her natural mother) to roam and chew on her beloved tennis balls. Mark's sense of belonging continued to increase as he invested wholeheartedly of himself to make the new house truly a home. He helped with every aspect of the move, wiring the electronics, and giving of himself in numerous ways. With each passing day, Mark grew increasingly more confident that he was a valued member of his own family.

All was not peaches and cream during this season. Mark came face to face with the impact of his past choices. He found that rebuilding trust in some key areas of life would take time. Linda and I were looking at updating our will and creating a family trust leaving our inheritance to Mark. We were not rich by any stretch of the imagination, but wanted to guard against Mark having a relapse, so we built in some conditions that would have to be met before he could assume full ownership of all assets. We involved Mark in this process, which created some hurt feelings on his part as he felt that we were not showing him much trust in light of all the progress he had made. We struggled through rewriting the documents as Mark began to understand that total trust takes time to reestablish and that there is always a cost for the choices we make in life. The very fact that we could address this sensitive subject with one another shouted volumes for the progress we had made as a family.

Mark received some more good news: he was able to change work locations and receive a promotion in the process. The new position included a benefit package that would allow him to obtain professional counseling and prescription meds at affordable prices. This was critical as Mark was fast approaching the final stages of completing his methadone treatments. Truly he was taking those slow but steady steps towards personal and emotional wholeness. We were so blessed as a family.

> Lessons Learned/Relearned: Power of Grace Over Judgment = "seeing how God has been working in Mark, Linda and I since we have brought him back home one and a half years ago – seeing how Your love/healing is working wonders in each of us – we are truly blessed by Your awesome love/grace to us in Christ and we have seen the healing power of sharing that with Others"
>
> (Prayer Diary: 6/12/04)

By mid-year, Mark completed his methadone treatments and was no longer dependant upon this drug substitute. This was a huge victory for him and gave him a tremendous sense of self-worth and accomplishment. About three weeks later, Mark was tested in his new-found freedom. Mark and I took a mini vacation together during which I dropped him off with friends for a few days while I spent time at a national book convention. This was a huge trust issue for all of us. Could Mark stay clean around his friends and resist following that all-too-familiar pattern of not being able to handle success on a sustained basis? Though we had kept in touch by phone, I was extremely anxious as I drove the one hundred miles to pick him up from a friend's house. What would I find? As I pulled slowly around the corner, there he was, sitting on the front porch in an old lawn chair with a big grin on his face. We hugged in greeting and then began the five-hundred-mile trip back home. As we drove down the freeway, Mark opened up and shared his entire visit with me. He was most thrilled that his friends, who had been so concerned with him a few short months ago, now saw him clean and reflective of that special person they all so deeply cherished.

When life is going smoothly, it is an extremely easy thing to become comfortable in the day-to-day activities and become less aware of the ever-present battle at hand. Mark's transition from the methadone treatments to prescription drugs did not erase the deep dependency he had developed over the many years of believing he needed something in his system to deal with life on a daily basis. Initially everything appeared to be going according to plan. Mark was seeing a counselor, using only prescribed medications, and managing his daily dosages. At the same time, he continued to find ways to secure what he called "recreational supplies" of marijuana; nothing Linda and I could do or say would deter him from this stubborn determination that he needed "Mr. M" in order to confront the perceived stress in his fragile world. We continually tried to help Mark understand that he would find much more joy in life by cultivating healthy friendships that would come alongside him and support him in "doing life" in a positive manner rather than constantly leaning on some type of drug to give him confidence.

A few weeks later, after doctors conducted some much-needed routine physical tests, an X-ray identified a spot on one of Mark's lungs. This new threat brought him face-to-face with his own mortality and the price of life choices, which to date had cost him no major physical concerns. Fear of what this could mean opened Mark's heart up to long discussions about prayer and God's work in our lives. It is amazing how much more open we are to God and counsel from others when we find ourselves in times of uncertainty. About thirty days later, Mark received word from the doctors that the spot was not malignant. He just needed to stop smoking and take better care of his body. Once again, we were blessed by the continued evidence of The Father's grace to this family.

Mark continued "doing life," confronting the stress it contained in his own strength, mixing in the support from his prescriptions and "Mr. M." We simply had to chose our battles and in prayer leave such choices in God's hands. There was so much for Linda and me to be proud of in our son during this season together. During this somewhat tranquil season, Linda suffered what we initially thought was a heart attack. Mark immediately flew to her bedside making sure the doctors and nurses were paying close attention to every minute detail. In other situations, he would provide valuable help with friends and family whenever asked. We began the first of several Thanksgiving family gatherings in our new home. We may not have agreed with some of his perceived dependencies, but it was hard not to love the way he made total effort to add value not only to his own life, but to the lives of his aunts, uncles, and cousins as well.

Unfortunately, Mark's life began to unravel as the challenges of the responsibilities of life chipped away at all of his hard-won progress. First was the struggle to manage control of his charge card in a day when credit was given out so freely. Mark had found another substitute for his old habits and relationships. He began to frequent a local pub and establish a friendship base from the other regular attendants. While he was forming this new circle of friends, he ran up a sizable debt and found himself falling behind in his monthly obligations. This led to calling a family meeting where I agreed to help Mark create budget accountabilities and begin to, step by slow step, manage his way out of debt. To help address this issue, Mark was to secure a second part-time job. In a couple of weeks he was hired to work a few nights delivering for a local pizza shop. On the surface, this appeared to be the right step to take under the current circumstances. However, it turned out to be a very catastrophic choice for all of us. In taking the job, Mark soon found himself drawn to other struggling individuals who were very much like those he had left behind those brief, precious thirty short months ago.

As these changing dynamics took root, Mark began to evidence another area in which he was fast losing control. For over a year, Mark had traded in his methadone treatments for prescription drugs. He was managing his own daily dosages during this time as well as seeing a professional psychologist. One day following his appointment, the doctor changed one of his medications; Mark had a bad reaction to them. He began to lose control of his sense of reality and drove his car into a deep ditch near the house. I hurried home from work following a frantic call from Linda only to find Mark backing his damaged car down the driveway in such an erratic manner that he almost hit the house. I had to forcibly remove him from the car and take his keys from him until he could sleep off the effects of the drugs. Following this episode, Mark agreed to let me provide the control for his daily dosage in a proactive effort to regain control.

While Mark struggled with regaining lost ground and restoring balance in his life, another cousin asked him to be an usher in her wedding. This is just what he needed:

a chance to give back and to feel a sense of being valued. Mark was excited at this opportunity to do something for his family and quickly secured time off to make the out-of-state trip. Linda and I drove separately because Mark, due to differing work schedules, had to leave a couple of days later. We worried much about him as we had to entrust his daily medications into his own care for several days until we united on the day before the wedding. Everything proceeded as planned. Mark arrived safely and began to enjoy this special time with his cousins. However, things suddenly began to turn sour at the reception following the marriage ceremony. Mark was determined to make the most of the free drinks being served; this, combined with his new medications, was a recipe for disaster. Mark was drifting in and out of consciousness as he quickly guzzled one drink after another. I tried to quietly pull him aside to ask him to stop drinking and allow me to take him back to where he was staying. Mark became angry. He dug in his heals and stated he was going nowhere. After much struggle, he finally allowed me to drive him back as he ranted and pouted the entire way. As I dropped him off at his room, my heart ached for him and I wondered where this was taking our family. Frightful visions of the past began to fill my heart. *Oh God, please, not again!*

In his anger, Mark did not stay the night, but determinedly put his dog, Meg, in the car and started for home without telling anyone. We finally heard from him around noon of the following day as he, full of pride, navigated his way angrily back home. There was no word of apology for the actions of the night before, just a silent determination to do life his way on his own terms. We held a family meeting once Linda and I arrived back home, seeking to help Mark understand the impact of his actions. Mark was not very receptive and began to withdraw more and more into himself. I even tried having man-to-man, heart-to-heart, point-blank talks with him, but he was just not willing to open his heart's door to listen. Truly the weeks leading up to this were fast becoming a terrifying reminder of the past that had ripped our family apart. We prayed that they were not a prelude to another painful season for our still healing family.

Matters became even more strained a couple of weeks later when Mark's doctor reduced his prescription dosage. This served to add more pressure to his strong belief that he required more medical support, not less, to deal effectively with life's daily challenges. Linda and I encouraged Mark to seek some type of support group of people who could better understand his thought process and corresponding cravings. He needed friends in his life who could directly relate to what he was experiencing daily. In answer to our prayers, God sent many caring people across Mark's path seeking to befriend and encourage him, but in the end he rejected them all. One of Mark's greatest passions, outside of "Mr. M," was music and specifically music production. Mark was gifted musically. He could play guitar, piano, and drums, had a great ear for sound, wrote songs, and could sing. He was very blessed with outstanding talent and a member of our church production team asked him to join the sound production group. As usual, Mark found a way to reject this opportunity and stubbornly pursue his own solutions in his own determined way.

We were struggling to balance the tensions of Mark's current mindset with times of incredible closeness. We comforted and prayed for one another seeking better solutions than those we had used without result in the past. In all of this, Mark still remained focused and proud of his job, which he had now held for almost two years. One time he did come close to losing it because of tardiness, but to his credit he squarely faced the discipline of his employer and was never missed a starting time again until the final days of his life. He was truly trying to fight the good fight, but unfortunately he was not taking a firm hold of the love and support being offered him. Again, he had to address his problems in his own way.

As Mark balanced his day job with his evening pizza delivery job, he suffered another reaction to his prescribed medicines and once again we had to create more accountability to protect him from himself. Once the effect of the meds had worn off, Mark apologized and expressed his deep sorrow at the danger he had put himself in as well as the anxious moments he had again put Linda and me through. In this latest occurrence, Mark had totaled his car by again running it into a deep ditch just outside of our subdivision and was very fortunate not to hurt himself seriously. Linda then was forced to take Mark to work each day prior to going to her own job until we could locate a cheap replacement for his car. As Mark's debt load continued to grow, he did fully apply himself to both jobs in a valiant effort to claw his way out of the deep pit he had dug for himself. All of us prayed that these latest events were just a brief snag in the long road of progress that Mark had trod for almost three years. In spite of our constant desire to hope for the best, there was that nagging voice of fear echoing loudly in our hearts that we were headed for much more desperate times.

By this time, Mark had completely stopped attending church with us. Summer was now passing into fall and Mark was struggling with virtually every area of life. His replacement car was in need of constant repair. He was putting on a lot of weight and his health was suffering from the long years of abuse and lack of physical discipline. None of these things were helpful in maintaining a positive self-image. Linda and I continued to spend hours with Mark over steamy cups of coffee frantically seeking to come alongside of him and encourage him in building upon the tremendous success of the past three years. For all of the heartfelt attempts each of us were attempting, Mark could not completely open his hearts door to receive the help he so desperately needed and we so desperately wanted to give.

> Wish I could go back
> To do it so differently
> Inside and out
> You could have carried me

> I passed you by
> Or did you pass me
> Did I say the wrong things?
> Is that why I am so empty?
>
> I couldn't tell you
> It left me wide open
> For pain I didn't need
>
> (Mark Brethauer)

As we began to prepare for our annual Thanksgiving gathering, Mark continued to withdraw deeper into himself and make short-term decisions focused on bringing fleeting pleasure for the moment. He had almost completely stopped addressing his financial debt and reflected little concern in repaying us for the money we had loaned him to pay for his last two cars. At this point, we began to have discussions with Mark about moving out of the house. We expressed concerns about repeating the past and were looking for constructive ways to encourage him to take hold of life's responsibilities, taking real actions that would demonstrate he cared for others as well as for himself. The conversations became so intense that Mark broke down in tears and cried out, "This is my refuge; where would I go?" Amid free-flowing tears we shared an intense family hug and prayed to God for His wisdom and grace. Family arrived for Thanksgiving and a wonderful time of shared intimacies was enjoyed by all, except Mark. He spent almost all of his time in his room sleeping, coming out only to offer brief one-line comments and engage in a quick smoke. Something was definitely wrong, as time with family was one thing he cherished greatly. Very shortly we would learn just how wrong things had become.

Two weeks after Thanksgiving, I took a couple of days off to catch up on some projects around the house. On one of these days, I set up a breakfast with Mark so we could spend some extended time together after he completed his early morning shift and I finished with a scheduled appointment for a minor car repair. Just prior to leaving the garage, I called Mark to confirm our plans for the morning and he informed me that he was going out with a friend to locate a part to replace the damaged fender on his car. I was greatly disappointed at his blatant disregard for this time to which I thought we were both looking forward. My disappointment in the morning was minor compared to the turbulent feelings I was to have before the day was over. Mark did not come home as normal to take a brief rest before going to his second job. Late that afternoon I received a call from him. He was laughing foolishly with every other word he spoke. He acted as if he did not have a care in the world. I listened to what he was trying to say and a sinking feeling hit me in the pit of my stomach. I knew in my heart: he was back on drugs! I confronted him over the phone about my feelings and he jokingly admitted that he and a couple of friends had gotten high. They had sideswiped another vehicle, but everyone was okay and the car was drivable. He would be home shortly.

As we disconnected the call, I felt so empty and hollow inside. I shared the conversation with Linda and through anguished tears we prayed for the safe return of our son. We saw every hard-fought step of the tremendous progress he had made slipping away so quickly. Mark was again heading full steam forward on that terrible downward path that seldom knew escape. He had finally succumbed to that ever-present voice of "Mr. M" now luring Mark to his deadly companions: cocaine and heroin.

Mark slept through the following day, so Linda and I were forced to put off talking with him until late in the day. When we finally convened as a family the words were honest, harsh, and hurting as raw emotions surfaced in our feeble attempts to address what each of us were feeling. Mark admitted that he was again struggling with drugs but insisted on handling his repeated dependency by himself, in his own stubborn way. We pleaded with him to explore attending a drug support group or better yet checking into a home where he could receive personalized assistance until he was ready to handle life. He rejected these ideas with his old prideful and determined heart. His only plan was to stay with us and deal with his problem in his own way and on his own terms. As suddenly as a flash of lightening across the midnight sky we had slipped back ten years in time. We saw ourselves staring into a very bleak future. *Oh God, we need you so much, there is no way this family can endure another season of such heartbreak.* God heard the desperate cry our souls expressed that troubled night and in less than six weeks we would know His challenging answer.

We spent an uneasy Christmas together seeking to capture the meaning of the season while facing the mounting trials and working hard to show love to one another. We had located a local ministry run by an ex-addict that took in five to six men for as long as needed to prepare them to do life on their own following becoming drug-free. We connected Mark with him and they set up an appointment to meet and discuss the next steps. In keeping with his "I can do it on my own" approach to life, Mark failed to keep any of the scheduled appointments. We continued on this way into the next year. It was evident that Mark was trying hard to overcome his addiction, but he was trying to do it all in his own strength. He even came to church with us one Sunday, and in God's perfect timing, the message was on the Prodigal Son and the Heart of the Father. This was the last time Mark was to attend worship with us.

Mark fought the valiant fight, continually seeking to overcome the addiction to heroin on his own. He would go days without using, only to lose the battle in the end. He would frantically seek out counselors and friends to support him, but could not bring himself to fully surrender to the accountability and drastic life changes that were required. It is so hard for a parent to watch their child coming apart from the inside out and not be able to do anything but love them. We continued to bounce from hard, tough-love conversations to times of great tenderness.

One night Mark did not come home at all. We didn't know if he even made it to work the next morning, but he was in his room and still sleeping when I arrived home after a particularly hard day at work. I knew in my heart that he had been out with his drug friends the previous night and was sure that he was soon to lose the job he had held for the past three years. I knew I needed to confront him. It was time to bring this craziness to a head before something more serious occurred. As I headed downstairs to do my nightly run on the treadmill, I bumped into a groggy, just-coming-to-awareness son who was in no mood to have a heart-to-heart family discussion. I decided to go ahead with my plans to exercise rather than become entangled into another pointless argument that would only serve to increase everyone's anger meter. We had learned that nothing constructive can come out of trying to deal with serious issues when both parties are not in an emotional state to listen. I finished my exercise regimen and was headed slowly up the basement stairs when I sensed God softly whispering to me to go and talk with Mark. I argued within myself that this would do neither of us any good and it would be best to wait for a more opportune moment. I started back up the stairs, looking forward to a much-needed shower, when I felt God's voice impress me much stronger than before: *Go and speak to your son.* Grudgingly, I made my way back down the wooden stairs and hesitantly opened the side door leading to the garage where Mark was smoking in stoic silence. The conversation started much the way I had envisioned, as neither one

THE SECOND CALL

of us was actually listening to the other. I don't know how it happened, but all of a sudden we were really connecting in meaningfully, honest discussion. The conversation was becoming very real and transparent. Mark shared in desperation that we didn't have a clue about what he was going through and how hard it was to be rid of this nasty parasite that was squeezing the life out of him. All I could say in response was that we could only imagine at what he was going through and try to come alongside of him in loving support. We did understand one thing: we had to do something and do it now! All of us! He responded, telling me that this was it, he was going to buy no more drugs and that he would work with us to take whatever steps were necessary. As I turned to go upstairs for that long-delayed shower, Mark, in his gravelly voice softly said, "Dad." As I turned to face him, he reached out with a big bearish arm and hugged me saying, "Dad, I love you." I hugged him back and whispered in return, "I love you too son." These were the last words that Mark and I shared with each other. *Father, I thank you for this precious moment. Your grace is beyond words.*

the Third
CALL

THE THIRD CALL

This last call came while I was at work during the afternoon following the open-hearted words that Mark and I had tenderly shared the night before. I was in the midst of an intense three-day process-reengineering workout session, when I felt my silenced cell phone vibrate. I opened the phone to take the call and I knew with Linda's first painful syllable that something tragic had happened. I will never forget the heart-piercing anguish in her voice as she tearfully wrenched the words, "I think he's gone; Mark's dead!!" From that first shocking moment I moved in dazed disbelief, not conscious of what I was saying or doing as I somehow made my way numbly to my car. Tears streamed down my face as my mind sought to take hold of the tragic reality of the moment.

In tear-filled silence, I drove home and pulled slowly into our driveway, which was crowded with police cars, county officials, and an ambulance. I made my way down the same basement steps that I had so joyously walked up a few short hours before following that tender moment Mark and I had shared. Hot tears blurred my eyes as Linda and I clung to each other trying to find comfort in a world that had suddenly sky-rocketed out of control. The officers asked us to not go in the small bathroom where Mark had passed and wait until they were able to wheel him out to us on a stretcher. Linda kept painfully repeating over and over, "He was so cold, so cold." Linda had experienced what no mother should ever have to face: finding your beloved child lying still with a needle resting on the cold tile floor beside his stiff, silent form. We watched in shocked disbelief as Mark's body was guided slowly out of the house and into the waiting ambulance. With fear and tenderness I lifted the covering over my son's now frozen face, and my heart broke as I first glimpsed my departed son. We continued to hold each other, crying as the county coroner escorted his body to its next destination. Mark's words of the previous night rang in my numbed mind: "No more drugs, Dad. I am not going to buy again; I am finished with this." Truly his words were prophetic; he was through fighting this terrible battle that had been tearing at his soul for so long. God had said, *Enough, I am taking you home with Me.*

Linda and I began the painful process of calling our family and closest friends. We could barely speak a single syllable before breaking down. God, in His awesome loving kindness, began to immediately gather those closest to us, surrounding us with their comforting presence. That first night was the longest night of our lives! Sometime late in the evening or early dawn, Linda and I fell limply into our bed, holding each other tightly, crying and praying through the remaining night. Somehow, we eventually fell asleep and as we awoke to the first empty day without our son, God's peace had miraculously pierced our hearts. He had supernaturally ministered a deep assurance to our broken spirits that Mark was indeed with Him; one day we would be together again.

During the next few days, Linda and I, in dazed determination, made the heart-wrenching decisions that are an unfortunate part of laying a loved one to rest. Selecting

THE THIRD CALL

a casket, flowers, headstone, service music, and message, etc., etc. were choices constantly thrust before us, fiercely interrupting our grieving spirits. Somehow, with the constant support of God's presence and dear friends, in trance-like fashion, we moved through the week. We were blown away at the tremendous outpouring of love from every corner of our lives. Family and friends past and current flew in to help comfort us. There were so many flowers that they streamed out into the main hallway of the funeral home. I remember very little of the actual service even though God gave me some final words to share with all who attended the funeral. We still could not wrap our hearts around the sad truth: our dear son was gone!

The last of family and friends returned to their homes. Linda and I were now left to face the day-to-day challenge of living life without the physical presence of our son. An overwhelming sense of emptiness swept over us like a winter storm. The week prior was a blur of painful heartache, incomparable love from family and friends, mixed with the cold, hard reality that life continues to move steadily forward. The number-one memory of that week was the tremendous outpouring of God's compassion from the countless caring loved ones who were sent to wrap themselves around our breaking hearts. Another powerful remembrance were the words of a young lady who said she owed her life to Mark, as his words of loving encouragement and warning kept her from taking a similar path. There were many such shared stories reflecting Mark's gentle spirit and they helped remind us of what a loving, kind heart he truly had. Though it was impossible to understand why God chose to take Mark home with Him at this moment, the love He kept pouring out upon Linda and me protected our hearts from becoming bitter. Everything was so out of order! A son should not die before his parents!

God used a very dear friend of ours to speak precious words of comfort and peace into our hearts as we struggled with our grief and confusion. The night following Mark's death, God placed this incredibly insightful poem upon his soul. Amid free-flowing tears he shared this message straight from the heart of The Father:

MARK

We don't know why and probably never will,
Why God allowed a demon to possess you that wouldn't sit still
Whatever it was that lived deep, deep inside
Wouldn't come out, but continued to hide
It lived in your mind, but could <u>not</u> enter your heart
And there my friend is where I would like to start.

How maybe, just maybe, God chose to take you home,
So that the rest of us, the living, could be shown
How your death teaches us life,

THE THIRD CALL

Teaches us to be good friends, husbands, and wives.
For you were born and lived with absolutely <u>no</u> sin
Of attempt to hurt, abuse, or take advantage of other men.

Yours was a heart filled with love and compassion,
Special traits that are not always in fashion
You loved all of God's creatures, in all of God's land
And I hate and I hurt that your life had to end.
Because you were not only a very good friend,
But truly in God's eyes, a great, great man.

Mark, the demon can have your body, that indeed he stole
<u>But God my friend, will never let him have your perfect soul.</u>

(Terry Meder – 2/06)

the Last CALL

God's final call for Linda and I has yet to be issued, but until that life-altering moment, we continue to see God's incredible grace in the midst of tragedy richly poured out upon us. Not a single day goes by that we don't think of Mark and the tremendous gap that we now have in our lives. No more long conversations over steaming cups of coffee, no coming alongside of him to work through life decisions, no more cards on Mother's Day, no more family hugs and tears, no hope of grandchildren.... The list is endless.

But also endless are the countless ways God has powerfully showered His grace into our lives. We have sought to both take in and share what God does in and through us. Linda and I have been adopted by two wonderful young women; Mark has had a kidney walk and a book dedicated to him; he is the namesake of his cousin's first child; and we are continually approached by those who were touched through his life. Beyond count are the opportunities that God has given us to share His matchless grace in the midst of terrible circumstances. These are but a few of God's special moments continually pouring themselves into our lives at the very time they are most needed.

We do not have all the answers, or even many of them. We can only guess at what future tragedies the three of us may have been protected from as Satan sought to destroy this family. As difficult as it is at times emotionally, we have a deep peace within that God has given us strength for today and a blessed hope for tomorrow and forever in eternity. Linda and I take comfort in knowing that Mark hurts no more and is waiting on us. We have learned to celebrate

Mark's life, not his death, and God's incredible grace over many, many years of trial and triumph. It is living these truths on a daily basis that brings healing to our wounded souls. It is our hope that sharing our story will, in some small measure, help those who have experienced great loss in their lives begin to understand that God's grace is more than equal to bring healing to our hurting hearts.

As the hymn writer of long ago was able to proclaim upon learning of the death of his entire family, Linda and I can echo with him, "It is well/It is well with my soul."

In Christ, Jeff & Linda

"I no longer live, but Christ lives in me. The life that I live in the body, I live by faith in the Son of God who loved me and gave himself for me." (Galatians 2:20)

"The name of the Lord is a strong tower; the righteous runs into it and is safe." (Prov.18:10)

"Come to Me, all who are weary and heavy laden, and I will give you rest. Take my yoke upon you, and learn from Me, for I am gentle and humble in heart; and you shall find rest for your souls, for My yoke is easy and My load is light." (Matt. 11:28-30)

PERFECT TRUST

I may not always know the way
Wherein God leads my feet
But this I know, that round my path
His love and wisdom meet;
And so I rest content to know
He guides my feet where'er I go.

I may not always understand
Just why He sends me
Some bitter grief, some heavy loss,
But, though I cannot see,
I kneel, and whisper through my tears
A prayer for help, and know He hears.

My cherished plans and hope may fail,
My idols turn to dust,
But this I know, My Father's love
Is always safe to trust;
These things are dear to me, but still
Above them all I love His will.

Oh, precious peace within my heart;
Oh, blessed rest to know
A Father's love keeps constant watch,
Amid life's ebb and flow;
I ask no more than this; I rest
Confident, and know His way is best.

(Author Unknown)

Made in the USA
Lexington, KY
26 July 2010